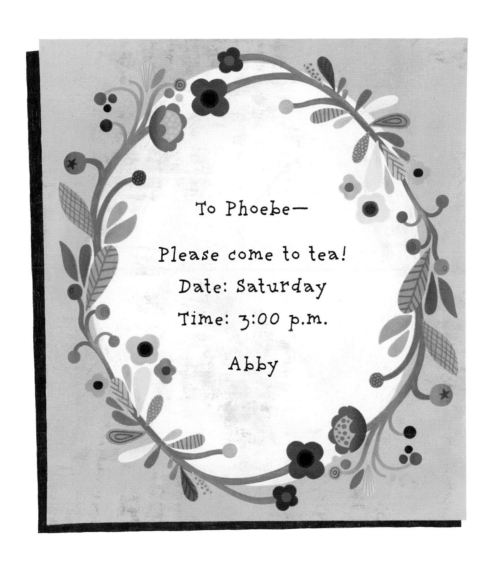

To Phoebe—

Please come to tea!
Date: Saturday
Time: 3:00 p.m.

Abby

THERE'S SO MUCH to do.
She'll be here at three . . .

PHOEBE DUPREE
Is Coming to Tea!

Linda Ashman

illustrated by Alea Marley

CANDLEWICK PRESS

Have you met Phoebe—Miss Phoebe Dupree?
Phoebe's as perfect as perfect can be.

Phoebe is speedy.
Phoebe is smart.

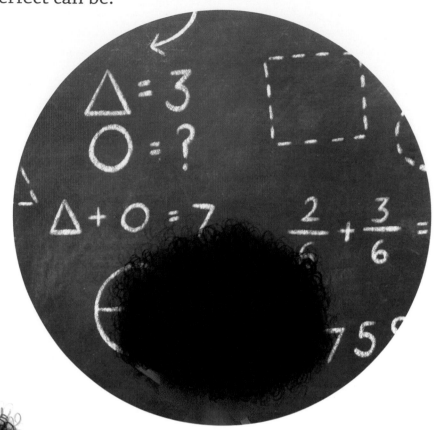

She's equally brilliant at science and art.

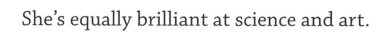

She sings like a bird (she's never off-key).

And Phoebe Dupree is coming to tea!

I bathe and brush Louie,
then lay down the law:
"You'll greet Phoebe nicely
with one gentle paw."

"You cannot go digging
or jump in the pool.

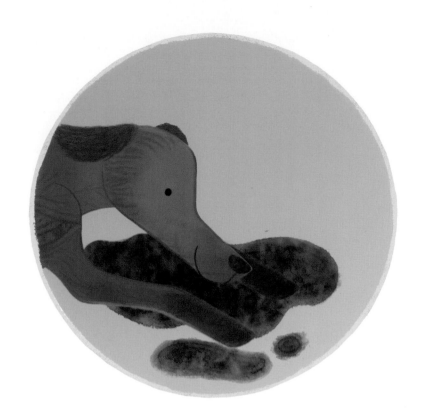

No barking.
No lunging.

No shedding.
NO drool."

We have to be perfect, beginning to end—
or Phoebe will *not* want to visit again.

I've layered a tray with tarts and éclairs
and lined up the guests—one doll and two bears.

I bring out the flowers, the china and tea.
Now everything's perfect for Phoebe Dupree!

I wonder what Phoebe is going to wear—
a flowery hat or bows in her hair?
Ruffles or polka dots? Yellows or blues?
Beads or a boa? What kind of shoes?

At last we're all ready.
It's just before three.
Then—

DING-
DONG!

the doorbell . . .

It's
Phoebe Dupree!

"Hi, Abby."
"Hi, Phoebe."
I welcome her in.

Louie bows sweetly.
She scratches his chin.

Then oh-so-politely,
she sits in her seat.
"Here, have some tea
while I bring in the treats!"

The tray's really heavy.
I'll make it—I'm strong.
Five steps and I'm shaking—
can't hold it for long.

Then right near the table,
the tray starts to slip.

It bobbles.
It wobbles.

I stumble . . .
then TRIP!

The cupcakes and éclairs
are tossed in the air.

Phoebe jumps up
and jostles a chair,
which rattles the table—
it teeters . . .
then tips.

She loses her balance—
the whole table flips!

"The teacups!"
"The cupcakes!"
"Your jacket!"
"Your dress!"
"What a disaster!"
"Oh, what a mess."

Then Louie runs in, all wet from the pool.
He shakes—and cascades us with water and drool.

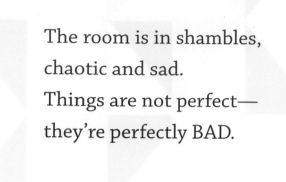

The room is in shambles,
chaotic and sad.
Things are not perfect—
they're perfectly BAD.

This tea party's over.

It's finished.

It's done.

"Oh," Phoebe says . . .

This is going to be fun!

She kicks off her shoes
and shakes out her bows.
She kneels to kiss Louie
smack-dab on the nose.

She picks up a cupcake,
presents me with half:
"Her Majesty's finest—"
then I start to laugh.

We rescue the treats—smushed but still sweet—
then sit side by side as we chatter and eat.

"This bear's wearing sprinkles."
        "There's glaze on the doll."
"The flowers are bent."
        "Do you mind?"
"Not at all.

"This tea party's perfect!" says Phoebe Dupree.

It's NOT how I planned it—
but still . . .

I agree.